Cosy Armchair Tales

Muriel Driver

Printed by The Lavenham Press

CONTENTS

Acknowledgments

With grateful thanks to

My family

Jeanette

Linda and Phil

Envelopes

"Late as usual," sighed Miss Geraldine Holmes.

"People knew how to make an appointment and keep to it in my day."

As Miss Holmes turned away from the window, she heard the scrunch of gravel and the screech of brakes.

Turning back, she stared in dismay as stones scattered across the petunia beds she'd lovingly tended all summer.

A man struggled to get out of the small white van. Once out, he slammed the door behind him.

He walked to the rear of the van, opening the doors wide. His feet tapping the gravel in time to the tune he whistled between puffs of his cigarette.

"He'll never change." Miss Holmes sighed.

She read the company name, 'Sparky Electrical' written in vibrant green lettering.

"*Well, at least it's ten out of ten for spelling and description,"* she thought.

The man looked across the garden, enjoying the colourful flower beds and lawns for a few minutes.

Picking up his toolbox he slammed both doors behind him.

Sauntering towards the steps to the front

door, he casually flicked the spent cigarette end onto the gravel, crushing it beneath his boot as he walked.

Molly, the Jack Russell, barked incessantly, jumping up and down in her agitation.

"Oh, Molly, DO BE QUIET, he'll be here in his own good time. No one has ever rushed Robert Sparkes." Miss Holmes patted Molly's head.

The doorbell rang and rang, as Robert Sparkes, known as Sparky to his friends, held his finger on the bell push.

Miss Holmes opened the door.

"I may be getting on in years, young man, but I still have perfect hearing and I'd thank you not to annoy either Molly or myself with that constant ringing."

"Morning Mrs Holmes," said Sparky, choosing to ignore her comment.

"Miss Holmes. It is MISS Holmes, as you well know," she sighed.

Sparky didn't seem to hear. Instead he said, "Put the kettle on and make us both a nice cuppa, there's a good girl."

Miss Holmes felt exasperated, yet she walked towards the kitchen to put the kettle on.

Sparky looked around the freshly cleared room, checking he had brought the correct number of brass sockets and light switches.

By the time Miss Holmes brought in a tray with two cups and saucers, a teapot, milk jug, and sugar bowl, Sparky had replaced one of the socket covers and was unscrewing the second.

"Any biscuits or cake to go with that cuppa, Mrs Holmes?" asked Sparky, grinning.

"I really do despair, young man. Will you never learn your manners?" said Miss Holmes. She fetched a plate of still-warm cakes from the kitchen.

As Sparky unscrewed the white plastic light switch in the hall, the letterbox clattered.

Envelopes fell onto the mat beside his feet.

Molly barked excitedly. "Do be quiet Molly," said Miss Holmes.

"I'll bring the post through as soon as I've changed this light switch over, Mrs Holmes," said Sparky.

Miss Holmes poured out the tea, placing both cups on the glass topped table between the chairs.

As she sliced the cake, Sparky walked into the room, holding out three gaily coloured envelopes.

"Golly, well it ain't Christmas, nor Valentines, so it must be your birthday! Happy Birthday Mrs Holmes."

"Oh, my goodness, let me see, third of August. Yes it is my birthday," exclaimed Miss Holmes, "Do you know, I'd quite forgotten – AND IT IS MISS HOLMES!"

"Come on, sit down and have your cuppa with me then, birthday girl.

How are you gonna celebrate your birthday then? Off up to town for a spot of lunch, or going to take in a show this evening?"

"I haven't thought about it. I have no family

to celebrate with and all my friends have either died or moved abroad to live in the sun. Well, all except Ethel next door and she's more a neighbour than a friend."

"That's a real shame, that is," said Sparky, rubbing his chin.

After a while, Miss Holmes said, "Do you know, I have been trying to work out how old I am. I think I must be eighty-five today! Eighty-five and I've never had a birthday party."

"Aw, that is so sad Mrs Holmes. My owd mum always put on a birthday party for us lot, every one of us, every year til we was twenty one, then we was on our own, so to speak."

"Well Robert, my mother died when I was born, you see, and I was sent to live with a horrid aunt. She treated me as a servant, not as a niece. I very much doubt she even gave my birthday a second thought, and so I have grown up not thinking about it."

"So who'll have sent the cards then?"

"I expect that will be Bert and probably one from Moira in Spain, and maybe Mary sent one from Australia.

Yes, see the stamps. I am right. They're the friends I mentioned. The ones who have moved abroad."

Miss Holmes opened the cards, read the verses and the note from Moira, then stood the cards on the piano, surreptitiously wiping a tear from her eye.

But not before Sparky spotted the

movement.

After the tea and fruit cake, Sparky continued changing the sockets and switches.

"Thank you, Robert. That looks much better and I am sure it is safer, isn't it?" said Miss Holmes.

"Well Mrs Holmes, I'm amazed something hasn't gone orf with a very loud bang before now!"

Miss Holmes gasped, as her hands involuntarily flew to her mouth.

The possible consequences didn't bear thinking about.

"I know. How about I picks you up and takes you to the pub for a birthday drink tonight. Let's say it's to make up for what a cheeky little bugger I used to be at school and all the hard times I must've given you." Sparky grinned.

"Oh, Robert Sparkes, that would be lovely, but not too late, mind." Miss Holmes was openly moved to tears this time.

"I'll picks you up at quarter past seven, then. See yer later," said Sparky, carrying the toolbox towards his van.

Miss Holmes waved out of the window as Sparky drove away.

"He'll never be on time, Molly. That's for sure." Miss Holmes patted the Jack Russel.

A thought was forming in Sparky's mind.

Pulling up in a field gateway, he took out his mobile phone and pressed numbers.

"Black Bull Inn, Springdown, how can we help?"

"Hello Ellen, it is Sparky 'ere.

You'll never guess what."

"Probably not, so get on and tell me then," sighed Ellen.

"I've just been up doin' some 'lectrics for Mrs Holmes."

"Oh Sparky, you know how much she hates you calling her Mrs Holmes. Why do you do it? It's MISS Holmes and you know it full well."

"Old habits, I s'pose. Anyways, listen. Like I was sayin', I've just been up there doin' some 'lectrics, and the post arrived. It's the old gal's birthday today. Eighty-five she is and not a friend around to celebrate with.

Just three cards from abroad, she 'ad. Poor owd luv."

"Oh, Sparky, that's so sad.

I hope I'm not like that when I'm that age."

Ellen's forehead wrinkled.

"What makes you think you'll get to be that owd?" Sparky couldn't resist.

"Cheek!" Ellen grinned.

"So, Ellen, d'you reckon you could put on a few bits of food an' lotsa balloons, an' maybe ask Don if he'll bring his guitar down and play. Say for about half past seven tonight? Oh, and will you ring Ethel Jarvis, tell her about the birthday. Ask if she can arrange to be at the pub for seven-thirty? Tell her I'll pay for her taxi when it drops her orf there, otherwise, I doubt she'll come. Tell her it's a big secret though and not a word to Mrs Holmes."

"What a wonderful idea Sparky. Sometimes you really do astound me. You're such a lovely chap deep down, aren't you? Quite a softie."

"Do be quiet, woman. You're makin' me blush!"

"I'll make sure there's quite a gathering here tonight, don't worry." Ellen hung up.

Sparky put the phone back in his pocket and drove home.

Ellen immediately made an announcement to the locals who were sitting in the pub. She asked them to spread the word, but make sure Miss Holmes didn't get to hear about the party.

At seven-fifteen sharp, Robert Sparkes, dressed in a black and blue striped shirt, black trousers and polished shoes, drove gently up Miss Holmes' drive.

Molly barked.

Miss Holmes looked out of the window. “Goodness, Molly. He’s cleaned the van.

Even more surprising is the fact that the hall clock is chiming seven-fifteen. He’s never on time, and, to the best of my knowledge, he’s certainly never been early,” said Miss Holmes.

Molly sat down in her basket.

Sparky turned the van around and parked quite close to the front door.

Miss Holmes opened the door just as Sparky reached out to press the bell push.

“Wow, you do look a right Bobby Dazzler. That dark blue colour do look great on you.

An’ is that gorgeous rose from your garden?” said Sparky.

“Of course it is. I haven’t been anywhere

other than here all day." Miss Holmes smiled broadly.

The taffeta gown rustled as she walked down the steps. The yellow rose, pinned at her tiny waist, added the perfect flourish.

Her lipstick had been painstakingly applied and her long, silver-grey hair coiled around her head like a tiny crown.

Sparky could hardly take his eyes off her. In all the years he'd known her, he'd never seen her without her hair in a bun.

"You musta driven the chaps crazy and set a few hearts a-throbbing a few years ago I reckon."

"Oh, I wasn't allowed out in the evenings, not when I lived with my aunt, but I always wished I could go to one of the dances in the hall," said

Miss Holmes.

Bowing her head slightly in recognition of his kind gesture, Miss Holmes lightly placed her hand on Sparky's proffered arm.

"*I can hardly believe this is happening,*" thought Miss Holmes, as Sparky walked her to the van.

"Allow me, madam." Sparky said, opening the door.

"Careful now and don't crease that beautiful dress when you put your seatbelt on." Sparky gently closed the door.

"It is so kind of you to take me out for a birthday drink Robert. Not like the Robert of school days at all," said Miss Holmes.

"Oh, *that* Robert just needed to prove he

didn’t need anyone or anything, but he grew up and realised the past was all rubbish,” said Sparky.

“Why, I do believe you’re blushing,” said Miss Holmes.

Sparky grinned.

Parking as close to the door of the Black Bull as he could, Sparky walked around and held the van door open for Miss Holmes, once more offering his arm as they walked into the pub.

“Oh look, what a surprise, there’s Ethel from next door. I didn’t think she ever came to the pub,” said Miss Holmes, still holding onto Sparky’s arm.

“Oh my, look at those pretty balloons. Several of them say Happy Birthday. I wonder who else here has a birthday today?”

From behind the bar, Ellen rattled a spoon against the counter.

The signal for everyone to come out of hiding.

There were shouts of "Happy Birthday" and "Surprise" as about thirty locals walked in from the next room and started singing.

" Happy Birthday to you

Happy Birthday to you

Happy Birthday Miss Holmes

Happy Birthday to you"

"Three cheers for Miss Holmes. Hip Hip HOORRAYYY, Hip Hip HOORRAYYYY, Hip Hip HOOORRRRAAYYYYYY!" said Sparky.

Everyone cheered loudly.

Miss Holmes took a handkerchief from her

midnight-blue taffeta bag and gently dabbed her eyes. “How kind you all are,” she said.

“Here you are Sparky. I hope these are what you wanted.” Ellen handed Sparky a very large and colourful bouquet of summer flowers.

Handing the bouquet to Miss Holmes, Sparky said, “Happy Birthday, MISS Holmes, we all hope you have a very special evening with us tonight.”

Miss Holmes threw her arms around Sparky. She gave him a firm hug and kissed him on the cheek.

Wiping her eyes again, she said, “Geraldine. My name is Geraldine. How can I ever thank you, Robert?”

Sparky’s bright face grew even redder.

"Why don't we have something to eat?" he said, pointing to the wonderful spread Ellen had laid on.

"This is simply delightful. I'm glad I've never had a birthday party before, because none could compare to this." Geraldine's face lit up with a broad smile.

When the sandwiches and nibbles had been consumed, Ellen brought in an iced cake with flaming candles on top.

Sparky turned off the lights.

"You must blow out the candles in one go, Miss Holmes, and make a wish as you do so," said Ellen.

"I don't need to make a wish. I couldn't be happier than I am right now. Though I would like

you all to call me Geraldine from now on."
Geraldine took a deep breath and blew out the candles.

Sparky immediately flicked the lights back on and Don strummed his guitar.

Sparky held his hand out to Miss Holmes, "May I have the honour of this dance, Geraldine?"

Cold Call

Jacko, usually a very patient St. Bernard, looked lovingly at Ben.

“Okay. Enough of the big eyes. Let’s go walkies.” Ben stood up, folding the newspaper.

Tilly smiled. “That dog has you wrapped around his huge paw.”

Ben was attaching the lead to Jacko’s collar when the phone rang. “I’m right beside it, love. I’ll get it,” he shouted from the hall.

“Hello. My name’s Mike. How are you this

evening? Do you have a couple of minutes for a quick chat?"

"I do, but I'm not sure that Jacko will approve. I was about to take him for a walk," said Ben.

Jacko whined.

"I'll be brief," said Mike.

Ben listened without interruption as Mike gave a parrot-fashion speech about how fabulous his kitchen refurbishment company could make any kitchen look.

"Woof." Jacko was getting impatient.

When Mike had finished, Ben said, "I've patiently listened to you tell me how wonderful your firm is and how you can turn the two-by-three-metre space containing our cooker and sink into the kitchen of our dreams.

Jacko is standing with his legs crossed.

I'm sorry, but I really do have to go now. Would you be able to ring me back tomorrow evening?" There was a glint in Ben's eyes.

"Would seven o'clock be a good time for you?" asked Mike.

"Wonderful. Speak to you then." Ben hung up.

"Good lad, Jacko. Now we'll go for that walk." Ben opened the door and off they went.

Just before seven the next evening, Ben sat

by the telephone. A smile playing around his lips.

Promptly at seven o'clock the phone rang.

"Hello. It's Mike here. I'm ringing back as promised."

"Hello Mike. Thank you for calling back. I listened to your chat last night, though I must apologise for Jacko's bad manners.

Would you be kind enough to return the favour? Would you listen to me read my part for the Christmas play?"

For some odd reason, we were cut off.

Misunderstanding

Have you ever had one of those conversations you wish you'd never started?

It all began at the office this morning when Maria took cups of coffee outside to Dennis and his son James, the contractors working on the grounds.

Simon, Maria's boss, was having an underground telephone cable laid from his house to the office in his back garden.

As Maria circumnavigated the trenches, trying not to spill the coffee as she went, she jokingly said, "Hey, Dennis. I won't be able to bring you more coffee unless you provide me with a bridge!"

"That's no problem," Dennis replied. "I have one at home that I am not using. The wife will be glad to be rid of it.

James and I will nip home and fetch it as soon as we've had our coffee."

"A spare bridge is a strange thing to have kicking around their home, but each to their own," Maria thought as she walked back to the office, stepping over trenches.

A little later she heard Dennis and James roar away in their old truck.

Engrossed in the letter she was writing,

Maria jumped when the double doors of the office were thrown open, revealing an extremely red-faced Dennis and a sweating James standing in the doorway with what can only be described as the most enormous fridge she had ever seen!

"Where do you want it?" asked Dennis, puffing loudly.

"What has Simon asked you to do with it?" she asked, amazed.

Dennis replied "Simon didn't ask for it. *You* did when you brought the coffee out this morning!"

Shelving Mishap

Kerry carried the neatly ironed pillowcases, quilt covers, sheets, and folded towels to the airing cupboard.

"I can't believe how many we use each week," she thought.

Balancing them on one knee, Kerry opened the door.

"Whoa!" she shouted. With no warning she found herself flat on her back.

The linen was still in her arms, and a whole

mountain more covered her body.

Since the first week of married life, when Will had put up two very wonky shelves, Kerry knew he was no carpenter. However, Will had inherited many of his grandfather’s tools.

"It stands to reason that he ought to be better than I am at nailing pieces of wood together, doesn't it?" thought Kerry, not for the first time.

Laying there while recovering her breath, she remembered the day they'd moved into the house.

The airing cupboard had only one shelf, and that was about seven feet above ground level.

"It will be fine," Will had said.

Kerry, however, hadn't agreed.

"It's okay for you, but I'm vertically challenged. How do you expect me to put anything up there?" she said.

After a month of Kerry complaining about having nowhere to put the linen, Will dutifully made a timber shelving frame to fit the airing cupboard.

Except it didn't fit very well.

Mainly because he forgot to make allowance for the door frame and the water pipes.

So bits and pieces were hacked off the wonderful shelving unit until it fitted.

"I remember how disillusioned Will became,

and it fell to me to prop up the wobbly legs of the unit," Kerry smiled, still covered in linen.

So, frequently armed with copious amounts of linen, when opening the airing cupboard door Kerry had kicked seven bells out of the shelving frame to encourage it back into shape.

Today, however, the shelving took its revenge. It fell apart. Linen tumbled out in an unholy heap, knocking Kerry to the floor.

Picking herself up, Kerry placed piles of linen on the landing.

"Only one thing for it. I'm going to the shed. I'll need timber, nails, screws, and the toolbox," Kerry said out loud, though there was no one else in the house to hear her.

It soon became obvious that these items had been hidden to save Kerry from herself.

Her scowl slowly spread to a wicked grin.

"That leaves me with no alternative but to place the linen on the floor outside the airing cupboard. That means he'll have to step over the linen on his way to the bathroom," she thought.

However, Kerry knows that until she makes a trip to a DIY store, Will is going to happily continue stepping over the linen and the airing cupboard will remain empty for some time to come, except for the blankets and curtains on the top shelf.

Left At Home

The wedding invitation was for the evening reception, leaving them plenty of time to take a relaxed drive up to the hotel.

"I've packed the case and two suit carriers. That way, nothing should get too creased.

Would you put them all in the car, please, Sam? I'll wash up these breakfast things." Gina stood up from the table.

"If you've finished upstairs, I'll bring those down and close all the doors up there." Sam was already halfway up the staircase.

After about ninety minutes in the car, Gina said, “There’s a lovely cafe in that garden centre. Shall we stop a few minutes?”

“That sounds like a good idea. After a break, we can swap over. You can drive the next bit, and I’ll relax.” Sam flicked the indicator to pull into the garden centre car park.

After a mooch around the plants, pots and gardening tools, Gina and Sam each enjoyed a coffee and slice of Victoria sponge cake.

Gina drove for a couple of hours before they pulled off the motorway, heading for lunch in a small market town.

Arriving at the hotel at around four o’clock, Sam carried the suitcase and one suit holder. Gina took the other.

At reception, they booked in, collected the key and went to their room.

“Just about perfect timing, I reckon,” said Sam.

“I’ll unpack and check nothing’s too creased.” Gina unzipped the first suit holder and hung up Sam’s suit.

“I’ll have a shower,” said Sam.

“Okay. The sponge bag’s in the suitcase,” said Gina, unzipping the second suit holder.

“Sam! Don’t turn that shower on. We have a big problem.” Gina cupped her hands around her cheeks.

"What's up?" Sam rushed out of the bathroom.

"The second holder's empty. You don't have a shirt. I don't have a dress or any shoes.

You can't go in the T-shirt you're wearing, and I can't go in these tatty old driving shoes.

What are we going to do?" Tears ran down Gina's face.

"Where's the stuff that should be in there, then?" Sam gasped.

"I remember now. I hung my dress and your shirt on the back of the door, ready to put in the holder. I'd just laid the holder on the bed when the phone rang. It was Jen, saying Jilly had the baby this morning. In all the excitement, I forgot to pack the rest of the stuff. I'm so sorry. What are we going to do?" Gina was crying uncontrollably.

Sam grabbed the car keys. "Get your bag, quickly now. We'll dash into town to buy what we need."

"But the shops will be closing." Gina threw her bag over her shoulder, following Sam down the stairs.

"We'll find something. Don't worry." Sam strode out across the hotel car park.

"Aren't you even cross?" Gina ran to keep up with him.

"We don't have time for arguments.

Anyway, it wouldn't solve the problem, would it?" Sam pressed the key and the car lights flashed.

Luckily, the traffic was light, and they were in the town centre within a few minutes.

"It's gone four-thirty. Let's park on the central car park. More expensive, but closer to everything." Sam was already parking.

"The sign at the entry says it's free after three," said Gina.

Leaping out of the car, they ran across the car park to the High Street.

"I've no idea what shops are here now. It's been so long since I was here." Gina looked about, not seeing any clothes shops.

"Keep running. We don't have time to stop and look," Sam said.

"Sam. Isn't that beautiful?" Gina stood outside a charity shop, admiring a turquoise dress.

"In you go. Try it on as fast as you can." Sam almost pushed her through the door.

Gina was upset when she found out the dress was too big.

"Just a moment," said the assistant. She disappeared into the back, reappearing with a red dress and matching shoes. "Try this on. It only came in this afternoon. So we haven't had time to price it yet. If it fits, we can work out a price."

"While she's trying on the dress and shoes,

can you tell me if you have a white or pale blue shirt, sixteen collar, please?" Sam looked across at the rails of men's clothing.

The assistant trotted to a rail of shirts, removing two, handing them to Sam. "Use the other fitting room, just there," she pointed.

Gina came out, holding the dress and shoes. "It's gorgeous. I'll take them both, please."

Sam shouted from the cubicle, "And I'll take the blue shirt, too."

"Now, where did it go? We have a hairband with rubies and diamonds on. They're not real, of course, but it would look wonderful with that dress." The assistant headed off towards the hats and fascinators.

“Ah. Here it is.” She handed a pretty hairband to Gina. “Try it on. There’s a mirror over here.”

As Sam walked out of the cubicle, he saw Gina’s reflection in the mirror, and knew she’d have the hairband. It looked perfect in her long, dark hair.

“Right, let’s settle our debts and get back to the hotel,” Gina said, opening her handbag.

“As the dress and shoes haven’t been priced, shall we say thirty pounds for the lot?” The assistant looked enquiringly at Gina and Sam.

“Make it forty, and it’s a deal,” Gina said.

“Thank you so much. I’m so pleased I could help you.” The assistant beamed as Gina placed her card against the machine.

"C'mon, Cinderella, now we have to get back to the hotel to get ready." Sam held out his hand to take the shopping bags from Gina.

"On my way, Prince Charming," said Gina, kissing him on the cheek.

Gina and her outfit received many admiring glances and comments that evening. She felt like the most beautiful girl in the room, except for the bride, of course.

Gina and Sam danced the evening away, laughing and chatting to friends on the dance floor.

The band played their last song, and it was time for everyone to say goodnight.

As they walked up the staircase, one of Gina's shoes slipped off.

A young man behind them picked it up, saying, "This is a true Cinderella moment. Allow me." He held out the shoe for Gina.

Thanking him, she placed her foot inside. "The real Cinderella had one Prince Charming, but I'm lucky enough to have had two Prince Charmings in my life today," she smiled.

Bath of Dreams

Almost mechanically, Abbie lifted her arms above her head, scattering fifty-pound notes into the air.

Cedric Greene spoke. “Well, Angela my love, we shall never again want for anything.

We shall live the rest of our lives in the lavish style to which I expect we will soon become accustomed.”

Abbie replied, “You made it all happen, Charles. Thanks to you and your wonderful invention we shall be rich and famous.”

Abbie sat in a bath. She was surrounded by hundreds of fifty-pound notes.

Not for the first time since the play started, she found herself wishing the notes were real, not theatrical props - Mickey Mouse money.

It was easy to believe they were authentic. They looked and felt like the genuine article, apart from the small fact that each note carried the same number.

As the theatre curtain slowly closed, laughter and applause sprang up from the audience.

Abbie stepped out of the bath, mindful not to lose the notes tucked into her shoes and pockets.

Silently the stage curtains opened again,

revealing Cedric, Abbie and other cast members standing, smiling, linking hands as they each bowed low to their adoring fans.

At last. The final night of the play, and this run was over.

When Abbie had first announced that she wanted to become an actress, it had been taken for granted that she and her twin sister would attend drama school together, applying for parts in the same plays.

That was why they had just finished a run in the most boring play in creation.

"C'mon, Sis. I can't wait to get home." Abbie almost ran to the bus stop.

"Hold on." Mandy struggled to keep up, as her new shoes hurt her heel and pinched her toes.

When the girls arrived at their less-than-chic flat, Abbie went straight to her room.

Flicking the light switch, she winced at the glaring lightbulbs.

Carefully avoiding the rucks in the cheap carpet, she crossed the room and closed the faded red velvet curtains.

The dreary curtains gave the room an old-fashioned air, making it look dingy and small.

"Attractive light fabric would be a huge improvement Perhaps light blue or minty green," Abbie thought.

But for now, she would have to live with these.

She lifted a shoebox from the top shelf of the wardrobe, placing it on the duvet.

"I hope I didn't lose any of these on the way home," she thought, taking the notes from her pockets and shoes.

Rolling them into bundles, she firmly secured each with an elastic band, and laid them alongside many others in the box.

For the first time in her acting career, Abbie was grateful that The Meldorian Academic Acting Company didn't wear costumes. Instead, they performed in their own clothes. It was felt that they were better suited to the plays of modern-day life than those in the theatre wardrobe.

Ever since the first full rehearsal, when Abbie had realised just how realistic the notes appeared, she made certain that she wore at least one garment with large pockets, and always shoes not sandals.

She always ensured that when her stage character, Angela, submerged herself in the bath, Abbie managed to stow some of the notes into her pockets and shoes before Angela emerged laughing.

The play had run for five nights with one matinee performance every week over the last six weeks. That made thirty-six opportunities to acquire fifty-pound notes to swell the shoebox.

Abbie had big plans for the money.

She wanted to thank her parents for all the hardships they'd endured whilst putting both sisters through drama school and for their support ever since. Now, at last, here was the opportunity to say, "Thank You."

"Tickets for a four-week stay with Mum's sister in Australia will cost more than I have in my bank account or the shoebox." Abbie sighed.

"It's high time Mum and Dad visited Auntie Jane. After all, none of them are getting any younger. Dad will be seventy-two in October, and Mum turned sixty-eight last week. Who knows how long they'll be fit enough for such a long journey?"

Replacing the lid on the shoebox, Abbie

lifted it back onto the shelf in the wardrobe.

"Tomorrow, I'm taking bundles of five hundred pounds into every bookmaker I can find in the city. I'll place bets on whatever takes my fancy. Then I'll sit back and wait and hope."

After changing her clothes and brushing her hair, Abbie went downstairs to help Mandy prepare a delicious dinner of Macaroni Cheese and Sticky Toffee Pudding - their favourite celebratory meal. The last night of a play was always a night for celebration.

After dinner, the girls watched a quiz show, shouting answers at the screen as they finished their Chardonnay.

At bedtime, Abbie lifted down the shoebox.

Counting the notes into heaps of ten, she placed an elastic band around each bundle and popped six bundles into her handbag.

She returned the remainder to the shoebox, closing the lid firmly and placing the box back in the wardrobe.

In the morning, Abbie rapidly washed and dressed.

"Hopefully Mandy will find my scribbled note by the kettle," she thought.

Abbie slipped on her shoes, threw on her coat, and slipped her handbag over her shoulder.

She almost skipped along to the bus stop.

While travelling towards the city, Abbie

smiled at the thought of her mother's face when she finally met Auntie Jane again.

The bell dinged for her stop.

Stepping onto the pavement and turning left, Abbie walked to the first of the bookmakers she came to.

Nervously, she filled in her form. *"I think I'll try Golden Boy."*

She handed over the form and money. The assistant counted the notes, barely looking at them.

Trembling, Abbie continued down the road, not allowing herself to think about the deceitful, illegal act she was committing.

She placed five-hundred-pound bets at each

of the bookmakers she visited that morning.

Spotting a cafe and thinking it was lunch time, she realised she hadn't eaten yet today, so she walked in.

"I'd like chicken curry and rice. Then I'll have a slice of lemon meringue pie with cream for dessert, and a cup of coffee please."

Abbie amazed herself by being relaxed enough to eat the flavoursome lunch.

"The last race will run at four-fifteen this afternoon. That gives me time to pop into a travel agent for brochures, and I'll look at the curtains in Dilly's."

Slowly, Abbie retraced her steps to the

betting shops, wondering what chance and fate had made of the 'money'.

On the bus home, she reflected on the time spent in town.

This morning she had parted with bundles of printed paper. This afternoon she was returning home with a pair of pretty green curtains and twenty-two thousand, two hundred and thirty-seven pounds in real money.

Of course, she hadn't won all the bets, but she wasn't disappointed.

Once through the front door, shouting a brief, "Hello Mandy," Abbie ran up the stairs to her room.

Swiftly closing those horrid red curtains, she vowed she'd replace them with the new ones before bedtime.

Placing the real money in a beautifully carved box of cherry wood, she thought, *"It only seems like yesterday that Lauren gave me this box for my twenty-first birthday. If only she knew what treasures it would hold."*

Locking the box, Abbie placed the tiny silver key on a chain around her neck.

After successfully fielding all Mandy's questions about where she'd gone and what she'd been doing all day, Abbie fetched down the new curtains to show her.

Mandy agreed that they'd make the room

look much brighter.

Abbie suggested going into town to watch a film, followed by a pizza at Antonio's.

Mandy readily agreed.

The sisters watched a swashbuckling romantic comedy, with their favourite man of the moment playing the handsome hero.

Later, over one of Antonio's superb pizzas and salad, they discussed the film and the heroine's dubious acting ability.

"I'm certain that we'd both be much better in the part," said Mandy, grinning.

Abbie smiled. "He'd definitely make a better stage husband than Cedric."

The girls laughed.

Once back home, Mandy heated milk and Abbie spooned drinking chocolate into matching flowery mugs.

They ate cookies and drank their hot chocolate while still discussing the film.

Eventually, it was time for bed.

Mandy fell almost immediately to sleep. Abbie could hear the comforting noise of her sister's regular snoring coming from the next room.

After a further couple of hours looking through the holiday brochures, making notes and working out costs for the holiday of a lifetime she would book for her parents, Abbie turned off her bedside light.

The snoring duo slept soundly through the night.

Abbie put out her hand and pressed the button, silencing the insistent ringing.

Sitting up, yawning, she prepared to start another day at work as the deputy editor of a popular magazine.

She saw three fifty-pound notes on her bedside table.

"Oh yes. Mandy popped in last night to pay her share of the rent."

Abbie scooped up the notes, putting them in her handbag, along with her share of the rent.

"I'll go to the bank today and get that paid in," she thought.

"Abbie, I had the strangest dream last night. I think we'd won the lottery, so we sent Mum and Dad over to see Auntie Jane. Wish it had been for real," Mandy handed Abbie a mug of coffee.

"That's odd", thought Abbie, *"Last night I dreamed that I was in a bath, surrounded by hundreds and hundreds of fifty-pound notes."*

Remembering her dream and feeling guilty, Abbie took a large gulp from her mug.

The Battery

“I've had a real blonde moment today. (Sorry to all the blondies out there. All the blondies I know are equally as intelligent as the brunettes.)" Penny was on the phone to her mum, Daisy.

What have you done, love?" Daisy asked gently.

"Well, it was misty this morning. As I drove to the leisure centre in town, I put the car lights on. You’ve probably guessed what comes next.

I parked up at the leisure centre. You know my old charabang doesn’t have a beeper to signal when the lights have been left on but the engine has stopped." Penny fiddled with the pen by the notepad.

"Oh dear. This isn't sounding good," said Daisy.

"I spotted Pam, a friend from the keep-fit class, so I jumped out of the car and rushed over to chat," said Penny.

"It's all becoming clear," sighed Daisy.

"After class, I told Pam that I needed to get a card and birthday present for Jess, so I'd leave the car there and walk into town,” said Penny.

"Pam went off to get her click-and-collect order from the supermarket beside the gym.

That was when I realised I'd left my purse at home." Penny sighed.

"James was working from home today, so I rang him and asked him to bring my purse and a bottle of wine from the cupboard.

I thought I could give Jess the wine even if I didn't manage to get her a card." Penny filled in the squares she'd been drawing on the notepad.

"James is an understanding husband. I'm sure he was there in a flash," said Daisy.

"After a grumble and moan, yes, he agreed," said Penny.

“I thanked him, and said I'd take the wine to Jess and I’d be home soon to cook tea.

James waved as he drove out of the car park." Penny started drawing more squares on the notepad, pressing heavily on the pen.

"I said he would," said Daisy, smiling.

"That wasn't the end of it, Mum. The car door made a strange noise when I unlocked it. Anyway, I got in and turned the key in the ignition. Absolutely nothing happened. Total silence. Dead as a thingy.

“I didn’t know what to do,” said Penny.

"Oh no," said Daisy, sitting down on the chair, realising this was going to be one of her daughter's long stories.

"After sitting there for a minute, I rang James again and explained the situation." Penny turned pink, remembering how silly she'd been.

"I'm sure he rushed straight over to help," Daisy sighed.

"James grumbled some more but said he'd be there in a few minutes.

Luckily, the car beside me pulled out just as James arrived. So he pulled in beside me."

"That was fortunate, Penny," said Daisy, her finger tracing patterns on the table.

“I said, "My knight in shining armour. Thank you for coming to my rescue.” He mumbled something incoherent," said Penny.

"Well, he wouldn't be best pleased, would he? Being dragged away from his work twice like that," said Daisy.

"James connected jump leads, first to his, and then to my car batteries. He told me to wait until he'd started his car before starting mine," said Penny.

"I hope you did as he said." Daisy's finger continued tracing the invisible pattern on the table.

"I did exactly as he said, but it was still dead. So I said I may as well take the wine to Jess while he fixed the car.

As I left, James was muttering to the car

engine," said Penny.

"Oh dear. That's not a good sign," said Daisy, pulling faces at herself in the mirror.

"I delivered the wine and walked back to the car just as James got it started." Penny sighed.

"Wonderful, I knew he would," said Daisy.

"He said, *"Now, get in and drive home. Don't stop for anything on the way. The battery needs a bit of a charge. Anyway, as I'm here, I'll get us a Chinese takeaway."*

I told him he was wonderful." Penny pushed her fringe out of her eyes.

He watched me drive off. I think he was making sure I didn't stall the engine at the traffic lights.” Penny rolled her eyes to the ceiling.

“Oh dear. I do hope you didn’t,” said Daisy.

“No. I did as he said, and drove straight home and parked on the driveway," said Penny.

"Well done, Dear," Daisy smiled.

"Not over yet, Mum. I reached across the seat for my handbag and realised I'd left my bag, complete with house keys, in his car when I took the wine to Jess.” Penny bit her lip.

"Oh, Penny." Daisy frowned.

"I fumbled in my pockets in the vain hope that, just maybe, I may have put the keys in there. No such luck, but I did find my mobile.

I thought it best not to phone James again

though." Penny again turned pink at the memory.

"I should think not. He's probably had enough phone calls from you today." Daisy stood up and walked about a bit, phone in hand, hoping to relieve the cramp in her foot.

"So I took the car for a run to charge the battery. I visited another friend a few miles down the road. Meanwhile, James arrived home with a Chinese meal for two. And he ate them both."

"Good for him. He deserved them," said Daisy, smiling.

“Thanks for listening, Mum. Bye now.”

The Match

“We’re up early, so let’s spend a leisurely hour over Sunday breakfast, then amble along to the football.” Stuart handed Rosie a mug of steaming coffee.

“We’re here with time to spare,” said Rosie as they drove onto the car park.

“There seem to be more cars than usual, given that most of the players usually arrive bang on time or late.” Stuart checked his watch.

From the roadway, the pitch was obscured by the village hall, which doubled as changing rooms for the football and cricket teams.

"See you later, love." Stuart collected his sports bag from the car boot and strolled into the changing rooms.

"Good luck. Score a hat-trick," said Rosie, as she walked from the car park towards the pitch.

"There's a lot more noise than usual, too. It doesn't normally get like this until the match is well underway," thought Rosie.

Rounding the corner, she was amazed to see the match in full swing!

A cheer went up as the opposition scored a goal.

Their spectators were in a jovial mood.

A couple of the players from Stuart's team

shouted at Rosie and pointed to their wrists.

"I have no idea why they're so upset," she thought.

Stuart, meanwhile, burst from the changing rooms, the double doors banging behind him.

Flying past Rosie, he turned his head to yell, “We forgot the clocks went forward last night!”

Arguing In Public

When Pete arrived home from work, he said, "Come on, Cheryl, I'm taking you out to dinner. It's about time we did something for us.

Ring your mum, and ask her to look after the kids for a couple of hours."

"Hi, Mum. It's Cheryl.

Are you free this evening?

Would you be able to pop round and look after Robbie and Stacey for a couple of hours, please?

Great. Thanks, Mum. See you in about half an hour.

Bye." Cheryl closed her phone.

Pete rang the restaurant. "I'd like to book a table for two for seven-thirty, please. It's Mr Havers."

At seven twenty-five, Pete and Cheryl walked into the restaurant.

"Do you have a booking, Sir? The restaurant is quite full tonight," said the young man at the desk.

"Yes, I rang earlier and booked a table for two. The name's Havers," said Pete.

After checking the register, the young man

led Pete and Cheryl to their table in the centre of the restaurant.

The couple chatted for an hour or so about Pete's work, and what to get the children for Christmas. For some obscure reason, the topic then changed to Pete's shed.

Pete became quite vociferous, his dulcet tones raising several notches, as he said, "Why MUST you put your rubbish in MY shed? It's for MY rubbish, not yours."

At this point, it became obvious that several people had stopped eating and were listening.

The head waiter was walking towards Pete and Cheryl.

Cheryl, thinking quickly, flashed Pete a radiant smile, and said, “Oh, gosh, and what did Sarah say to THAT?”

Pete’s chin almost hit the table.

He quite simply said, “What?”

Hide And Seek

It was Katie's fifth birthday party. There were many excited squeals and screeches, as there always are at children's parties.

After games of Piggy in the Middle with balloons, Hide and Seek, and Musical Chairs, the next game on the list was Pass the Parcel.

Everyone was sitting nicely in a circle, waiting for the music to begin, when Jim said, "Where's Gemma?"

The children stopped talking and looked

from one to the other.

"She might have gone to the toilet, Mrs Walsh," said Casey.

"Good idea, Casey. I'll go and check." Lily ran upstairs to the empty bathroom.

"She's not here," Lily called out, retracing her steps with equal speed.

It became apparent that no one had seen Gemma since Hide and Seek. That was several minutes ago.

“Don’t panic, Lily. She’s here, somewhere. The door’s locked, so she can’t have gone out,” said Jim, reassuringly.

“Let’s have another game of Hide and Seek

but this time we are only looking for Gemma," said Jim.

Nine children squealed in delight. They ran from room to room, looking under chairs, behind the sofa, in Katie's bed, and behind the curtains. All searching for their friend Gemma.

"Oh Jim, we've searched everywhere. Gemma's nowhere to be found," said Lily.

"I think the monster may have taken her," said Katie.

"Don't be silly, Katie. You know there are no monsters here," said Jim.

Katie's face turned pale.

"Well, I heard a scary noise coming from

the cupboard under the stairs. It *might* be a monster," she said.

Two of the children started crying. Others ran to hide behind Jim and Lily.

"I'll look in the cupboard," said Jim, striding into the hall.

Everyone followed. Heads peeping out from behind Lily's back.

As Jim opened the cupboard door, they all heard the noise.

Children screamed.

Lily gasped.

"It's the monster," cried Katie.

"If it's the monster, it's asleep. I can hear

snoring," grinned Jim.

"I've already looked in the cupboard, but I didn't see her," said Lily.

"Come here," Jim beckoned.

Gemma had upturned the linen basket and was totally hidden beneath it.

The children started laughing.

Gemma woke up, wondering what all the commotion was about.

"Someone shone a torch into the cupboard, so I was extra quiet. I might have gone to sleep. Have I missed any of the games?" asked Gemma.

"Don't worry, Gemma. It's time for tea now, then we'll play more games," said Lily, smiling at

Jim.

As they walked to the kitchen there were yells of, “Yippee. Jelly and cake.”

Missing Letter

The rain stopped abruptly.

The sudden quiet seemed louder than the pounding rain had been.

Not even a car was to be heard. There were always cars travelling past, but not now.

"Probably a flash flood somewhere not too far away then." Carla was glad to be home in the dry. Though the quiet seemed eerie after the last few hours.

"I think I'll ring Sandra and make sure she

managed to get back from town okay." Carla dialled her friend's number.

After letting the phone ring for several seconds, Carla hung up.

"That's odd. Sandra said she wasn't going out again today for anyone or anything. I'll try her mobile."

Sandra's mobile rang and rang and rang.

"I'll send her a text. Sandra NEVER ignores her mobile, no matter what she's doing or who she's with."

Carla typed '*Hi Sandra, I've tried ringing, but you're not answering your land line or mobile. Let me know you're okay please. xx'*

After several minutes, and no reply, Carla began to worry.

She sent Sandra an e-mail. *"Hi Sandra, me again. I've phoned you on both phones and texted. Now I'm e-mailing. Will you just let me know everything is okay please? I'm worried about you."*

Carla flicked the kettle on and made herself a coffee.

Coffee finished, she thought, *"Well, I don't have any option but to ring her neighbour, Chris. I know they don't really get on that well, but this may be a good time to make up their differences and decide to be pals again. Needs must, anyway."* Carla looked up Chris' number.

"Hello Chris, it's Carla here, remember me from Terri's party? That's right, yes, I was the one in the green dress with black blobs all over it.

Look, I wonder if you could do me a big

favour. I know you and Sandra don't exactly see eye to eye, but I've been trying to contact her for almost a couple of hours now, and she said she was definitely going to be in. It's so unlike her not to even answer her mobile or reply to a text. Would you be an absolute angel and pop round next door to make sure she's okay please?

Yes, I know.

Yes, I'm really sorry to ask.

Well can't you pause it and continue watching it in about five minutes when you get back?

It's really important or you know I wouldn't dream of asking you. I just want to be sure she's not had an accident or anything.

Thank you Chris, I owe you.

Just ask Sandra to give me a call, that's all. Thanks again. Bye. Hope you enjoy the rest of the film."

Carla hung up, thinking, *"You selfish cow. Like having to pause a DVD is as important as the fact that there may be something really wrong with your neighbour."*

Flicking the kettle switch again, Carla opened the biscuit tin.

"Oh, only a three digestive biscuits left. Well I may as well put them out of their misery. Damn, half that one is floating in my cuppa now! It's never the same, eating a soggy digestive off a tea spoon, not to mention the floating bits in the cuppa.

Lordy me, that phone made me jump."

“Hello, Carla speaking.

Hi Chris.

You what?

Oh my God! So what have you done about it? Who have you called?

Have you any ideas at all? It’s so not like her.

Yes, I am worried.

Shall I come over?

Well, I suppose you’re right. There’s not much I can do, even if I do come over, is there? What about her cats?

Yes, I expect they’ll be alright for a few more hours.

Will you let me know if you hear anything, please?

Yes, I'll keep you posted if I hear anything.

Thanks Chris. I'm so glad I asked you to go round." Carla hung up.

"Where on earth is Sandra then? She's so reliable you could set Greenwich Mean Time by her. This is so out of character.

I think I'll wander up to the corner shop, get some more milk, and loo rolls," Carla thought.

She put on her thick green coat and looped the long blue scarf around her neck.

Picking up her purse and phone, she tucked them both into her coat pocket.

As she closed the door, she pulled woollen gloves onto her already chilling fingers.

"Oh boy, I am glad I put my big scarf on tonight. I don't think it would matter much if the

street lights were on or not, the moon's so bright there's no need for a torch.

Goodness me, there's a queue right out of the bookshop! What an odd time for it to be open," she thought.

Carla walked over to the queue, and approached a middle-aged lady, "S'cuse me, what's going on in there?"

The lady gave her a withering look.

"Well, assuming you can read, there's a notice in the window that's almost big enough to see," she said.

Carla glanced at the window. Indeed, the announcement almost obscured the entire window.

"Oh, yes, I see. Thank you. I didn't realise." Carla felt her face and neck glowing.

"Why had she kept this such a secret? HOW had she kept this such a secret?

So, here I am, standing at the back of the queue. What's the betting the corner shop will be closed by the time I get to it now?"

Carla pulled out her phone, and removed a glove.

"Hi Chris. I've found Sandra.

Yes, she's fine.

Thanks for your help."

The lady turned round.

"Sorry to disturb you." Carla smiled.

"You didn't disturb me. Apparently I have that sort of permanently angry-looking face. Oh look, it's starting to snow." The woman looked up at the sky.

Slowly at first, snowflakes ambled around with no sense of purpose.

Within a couple of minutes though, they gathered momentum.

By the time they reached the book shop doorway, Carla and the woman resembled snowmen.

There were gasps of joy or groans of despair from unsuspecting people coming out of the shop.

“I understand she’s from somewhere around here. I’ve always enjoyed her books, but only just found out she’s local. How about you?” said the woman.

“She’s a friend, and yes, she does live locally. I didn’t realise she was here tonight.

I was just on my way past, when you

pointed out that maybe I need an appointment with the opticians!

My name is Carla, by the way."

"Pleased to meet you Carla. My name is Hannah.

So how long have you known Sandra then?" asked the woman.

"We were in the same class at school together all the way through from the very first to the very last day."

"You must have lots of tales to tell, but they'll have to wait for another time. We're about to go into the shop," smiled Hannah.

As they reached the table where Sandra sat, Hannah said, "Hi Sandra, I was just telling Carla here that I'm one of your biggest fans. I was so pleased when I saw you were doing the signing tonight. Carla says you're friends."

Sandra looked up, startled.

"Hannah was just asking how you and I know each other." Carla smiled politely.

"Sorry Carla, I owe you an apology." Sandra looked down at the table.

Hannah felt rather sheepish, not sure which way to look, realising she'd upset a hornet's nest.

"I should finish signing for people. Maybe we can meet up for coffee tomorrow, if you'd like to." Sandra looked from Carla to Hannah.

"That would be great, Sandra, I've been looking forward to meeting you for a very long time." Hannah grinned.

"Well, now I know you're alright, I'll be off.

Maybe see you tomorrow. Let me know where."

Carla turned to go.

"Oh Carla, I'm so sorry. I didn't expect to be doing a signing here tonight, it all happened rather suddenly yesterday. I'll explain it all tomorrow.

Take a book now though, and tell me what you think."

Sandra told the lady on the till that this one was 'on the house'.

Turning the book over in her hands, Carla could hardly believe what she saw.

Sandra had written a cookery book with the most wonderful photographs of what were supposedly her own creations.

"They look fabulous, but there's just one

small, niggly fact. SHE CAN'T COOK TO SAVE HER LIFE!" Carla glanced back, but Sandra was busy, pen in hand, signing books for her readers.

Carla pulled out a carrier bag, and placed the book inside.

Her watch told her it was too late to fetch milk now. So she went home.

"Too late for milk, and too late to light the stove," she thought. Sitting in her cosy armchair, she pulled the crocheted blanket over her curled-up legs.

Opening the book, Carla read the first couple of pages, then flicked to the recipes.

"Hang on a minute, I recognise that recipe. It's one of my Mum's!

Mum collected these recipes, and wrote

them in exercise books. She gave them all to me when she moved into the flat about three years ago!"

Carla turned more pages.

"Well! Of all the nerve!

This has been one of my family's favourite Christmas recipes for generations."

Carla went to the drawer. The books were missing.

With a determined look on her face, Carla marched back to the shop.

No queue now. She headed straight towards Sandra.

All guns blazing, she didn't care who was around to hear the outburst that was about to ensue!

However, she was brought to a sudden and

grinding halt by the fact that Sandra was laughing and shaking hands with a very well known actor!

"What?!"

"Thank you so much for your very kind gesture, Sandra.

We all know that this must have taken an absolute age to put together, and we acknowledge the work and effort of Julie Farrant in collecting and testing these recipes during her life time."

"He was acknowledging Mum! He's still spluttering on." Carla's feet seemed glued to the floor.

"Once again, Sandra, from the bottom of our hearts, we thank you for donating all the profits from this book to the ICL. It's very much appreciated.

This money will make an enormous difference to a great many people who are reliant on the Injured Chef's League, and we appreciate that it's a charity very close to Julie Farrant's heart."

Carla looked from the actor to Sandra, then back again.

"What a wonderful coincidence. This is Julie Farrant's daughter, Carla.

Carla, I'm sure you'll recognise Jeffrey."

"Hello Carla. Thank you for allowing Sandra to use your mother's wonderful recipes in her book.

Whilst Julie has agreed to her recipes being used, I have yet to meet her, so it's a privilege to meet her daughter this evening.

We can't thank your mother enough for the

huge support the sales of this beautiful book will make to our charity." Jeffrey shook hands with Carla.

Not knowing what to say, Carla smiled.

"Why didn't Mum or Sandra tell me? When did Sandra take Mum's exercise books?" Carla's head was swimming with questions.

"Oh well, the cat's out of the bag now. Why don't we all go over the road and have a drink? Then I can answer the questions I know Carla must have," said Sandra.

"My treat," said Jeffrey.

Once everyone was seated by the roaring fire, Carla looked at Sandra. "Well?"

"Well. You know you asked me to pop in on your mum while you were working in America.

One day, she and I were talking about cooking, and she told me about all the recipes she'd collected, and that she'd given them to you for safekeeping when she moved to the flat.

I said they'd make a wonderful cookbook.

Long story told short – she said she'd like me to write it, and she'd like the book profits to go to the Injured Chef's League charity.

She came with me to your flat, we collected the exercise books, and the rest, as they say, is history." Sandra looked uncertainly at Carla.

"Carla, you can't begin to imagine what a boost this is to the charity.

Your mum suggested that, once you'd recovered from your travels, you and she could put on a cookery display in the mall, using a couple of the recipes from the book." Jeffrey flashed a charming smile.

"Your mum said she'd write to you, explaining it all," said Sandra.

"Well, she didn't.

Tonight is the first I've heard of any of it," said Carla, still feeling bemused.

After much discussion, Carla agreed to do a cookery demonstration alongside her mum.

"I told Hannah I'd be in Bella's Tea Rooms at ten o' clock in the morning. I hope you'll be there, too, Carla." Sandra hugged her friend as they left the pub.

Next morning, Carla's phone rang as she was eating breakfast.

"Carla, I'm such an idiot."

"What have you done, Mum? I need to talk to you anyway."

"I'm so sorry, Carla. I wrote you a long letter in August, but I've just found it in my handbag. I forgot to post it."

Carla smiled. "It's alright, Mum. I think I can guess what it said."

Bubble's Journey

A bubble floats over the new-mown grass, riding high on the gentle summer breeze.

Spinning quietly round and round, gliding silently through the air. Displaying the myriad spectacular soapy colours trapped within its walls.

The world below reflected hazily upon its spinning surface.

Now it sinks as if attached to a spider's web. Dropping until it nearly bursts upon the thorns of a pretty pink rose bush.

Settling for a moment, quivering gently upon the velvet grass as if deciding which way to go.

It sets sail again. Continuing along its meaningless journey around the earth.

A curious cat glances at the pretty air-filled bubble.

The excited cat races across the grass, under the hedge and into the next meadow.

Paws in the air, dancing.

Chasing the elusive bubble.

A breeze tugs the bubble hither and thither.

The cat loses sight of its prey and returns through the hedge and into the garden.

Lazily walking indoors it stretches out on the cooling flagstones of the farmhouse kitchen.

Ever onward the bubble gently glides.

Miracles and misdeeds of the lazy, sleepy world below shine around its glossy globe.

Translucent colours grow ever brighter as once more it swoops, hovering above a spiky plant, as if wishing to watch the butterfly drinking nectar.

The bubble basks a moment in the golden sunshine.

Then off again, floating high above the world.

A sudden, gentle gust forces the bubble downward.

Downward.

Too low.

A gentle PLOP awakens a slumbering dragonfly.

Looking around, the dragonfly sees no cause for the noise.

Bejewelled wings a-hover, it takes flight.

Impasse

Elana was driving through the next village, on her way to work.

The usual quota of cars and vans were parked on the side of the too-narrow street.

Elana sighed at the convoy of cars, led by an animal feed lorry.

Technically, the cars in her line of traffic had the right of way.

However, a foreign lorry driver travelling in the opposite direction thought otherwise. He, also leading a convoy, pulled out from behind the stationary cars, driving straight towards the animal feed lorry.

By now, there were probably twenty cars behind ‘Elana's’ lorry, and almost as many behind the other lorry.

"It's blatantly obvious that I'm going to be late for my client appointment at the office." Elana looked in the rear-view mirror and grimaced at herself.

Eventually, the foreign lorry driver realised his error and attempted to cajole his followers to reverse.

Horns tooted on both sides. This simply added to the utter frustration of all concerned.

As they were in a no-signal area, Elana couldn’t even let anyone know she'd be late.

A group of onlookers gathered, offering advice – some of it polite – to the lorry drivers.

After several minutes, the traffic moved.

"I can but hope the boss is in and is looking after my clients," thought Elana.

Driving onto the office car park, Elana sighed as she glanced at the dashboard clock. *"Twenty minutes late."*

She sprinted the few yards to the office, where she found her client standing on the doorstep.

"I'm so sorry. There was a massive hold-up on my route this morning. Do go in," said Elana.

"We'd love to, but the door's locked," said Mr. Thorl.

"Oh no. I expect my boss must be caught up in the traffic too."

Elana was dialling her boss when a young lady dashed past them all, keys in hand.

Red in the face, and puffing hard, the young lady rapidly unlocked the door, saying, “Hi, I’m Davina. Mum, Mrs Harris, and I were held up in traffic, so she asked me to get out and run to unlock the office.

You’d never believe the hassle we had getting through Lowstock village this morning”.

“Oh, I think I would.” Elana grinned.

Chocolate

“Natalie, lets go on a late autumn coach trip. I like the look of this one.” Henry passed the brochure to his wife.

October found the couple in a cold, wet town somewhere in Austria.

“I’m not staying in the hotel all week. Let’s get out there. Who cares about the weather?” Natalie threw a large umbrella onto the bed.

“It’s lucky you packed the ‘brellas, Nat.” Henry picked up the black brolly and put on his coat and boots.

Natalie packed the blue and lilac travelling brolly, her purse, two bottles of water and a fold-up bag into her backpack.

"Let's take the train. It'll be more exciting than using the trains at home." Henry grabbed her hand, pulling her towards the railway station.

"The views are fabulous. Look at that, Henry." Natalie pointed to a castle seemingly floating in a lake.

All too soon, their journey ended, and they were back on the wet streets.

"Brollys up." Henry released the button, and his umbrella flew up.

"You look like a male version of Mary

Poppins," Natalie grinned.

"As much as I love wandering around these Austrian towns, I think I'd like to find some shelter now." Natalie was beginning to wish she hadn't suggested coming out.

"Let's pop into this chocolate shop. They have free samples." Henry licked his lips.

"They're all delicious. We'll get some for Bev and Sandy, and for Lyn and Greg. Would your mum like some, do you think?" Natalie was already feeling for her purse.

"Just get one box for now. We can always come back for more, but there are lots of chocolate shops here. We have to shelter somewhere from this weather." Henry laughed.

Natalie and Henry spent a pleasant morning wandering from chocolate shop to chocolate shop.

"Goodness, it's lunch-time, but I don't feel hungry, do you?" Natalie looked at Henry.

"No, I don't, and it's not surprising, is it? How many choccie samples have we scoffed this morning?

Let's buy a few more boxes and then we'll head back to the hotel. The weather isn't going to let up." Henry pulled up his collar.

After another hour of wet streets and chocolate shops, the couple returned to the railway station.

"It's not been the best of holidays, because

of the weather, but it's not been bad, has it?" Natalie passed a bottle of water to Henry.

"I can hardly believe the week's up and we're on the coach for home again tomorrow." Henry looked out of the train window. Houses appeared to fly past. "These trains seem faster than ours, too."

The couple walked quickly back from the station to the hotel.

"Not the day for walking," smiled the receptionist as Natalie requested their key.

Back in the room, Natalie started packing, ready for their early morning start. "I'd like to get everything packed now, except tomorrow's clothes and the sponge-bag. Then we can enjoy dinner and watch the entertainment tonight."

"Good idea, Nat." Henry took his clothes from the wardrobe and piled them up on the bed, beside the open suitcase.

Not wanting their chocolate purchases to get squashed, Natalie packed the goodies into her capacious back-pack.

"I'll carry it." Henry placed the suitcase and back-pack beside the bedroom door.

"Almost seven. We'd better go down for dinner." Natalie checked her reflection in the full-length mirror before slipping on her shoes.

After enjoying bowls of moules frites, they chose Sachertorte then coffee.

"I think I've had a year's worth of chocolate today. I really should've ordered something unchocolatey for dessert," grinned Henry.

"Yes, maybe we should've chosen the Apfel Strudel," said Natalie.

"That magician must be in the magic circle, Nat. I've no idea how he's doing any of his tricks."

"He's brilliant," Natalie agreed.

After the show, the couple danced for a while.

"We'd better get to bed, Henry. It's only six hours now until we have to leave. The alarm clock will be going off before we know it." Natalie walked towards the winding staircase.

After a few short hours, they were on the coach heading away from the town.

Henry placed the back-pack of chocolate by his feet, not wanting it to be squashed on the overhead rack or in the hold with the suitcases.

All too soon, they were back in England.

The rain was as miserable as it had been in Austria.

With little to see except raindrops on the windows the couple looked at holiday photos on their phones and chatted to people around them.

Once home, the bag of chocolates was placed in the hall cupboard.

"Let's deliver the family presents at the

weekend," Natalie suggested.

"Makes sense. We're going to be too busy through the week," Henry agreed.

In the morning, Natalie took one of the gifts to their neighbour. A thank you for looking after Titan, their large black cat.

Henry took a box of chocolates to work, leaving them on reception for staff to help themselves.

After a couple of days, Henry succumbed and opened one of the boxes of deliciousness they'd brought back for themselves.

"Oh no. Natalie. Look."

To their utter dismay, instead of about

fifteen assorted chocolates, there was one marble-effect, misshapen slab!

"I hope the others aren't like that. How did it happen?" Natalie gasped.

They then realised that Henry had placed the bag of goodies by the heater vent in the coach, and so the chocolate melted. It had set again by the time they opened the box.

"I'm a total idiot," Henry shouted.

"The chocolate is unique, and it does look pretty," said Natalie, kissing Henry.

The attractive slices of assorted chocolate quickly disappeared, and no complaints were forthcoming from friends or family.

The New Shed

The new shed arrived. Flat packed.

Emily thought, *"This isn't going to be a fun-filled day. Now we have to assemble it."*

Graham, her brother-in-law, was enlisted to assist.

After a few trials and errors, the floor was down and the walls were up.

"Great achievement! Let's have a celebratory beer," said Jake.

"Let's get the roof on first," said Emily.

"We should, in case it rains." Graham

looked skyward.

"Okay. You're probably both right." Jake sighed.

"Emily, we need you to stand inside, and gently guide the roof as we lower it." Jake was already lifting his end of the roof.

There were two problems with this.

One: The shed is six feet high at the lowest point and even with arms outstretched, Emily couldn't reach that high.

Two: The boys were at the point of no return with the lowering of the roof before they all realised the truth of point number one.

Molehills

"I must empty those plant tubs. They need new compost, then I can plant them up for summer," Lou thought.

Emptying the soil into the wheelbarrow, she pushed it across the shingle and round to the garden.

"I'll tip it onto the flower beds." As Lou trundled the last barrow-load round, she thought, *"This is heavy work. I'll fork it in properly tomorrow. There was more soil in those tubs than I'd realised."* She wheeled the barrow back to the shed.

The kettle was just boiling when the front

door opened.

“Mum, is it okay if Ivy stays for tea?”

“Of course it is. You’re always welcome, Ivy. You know that.”

“Thank you, Mrs Wheeldon,” Ivy smiled.

Nicky gazed out at the rose garden. “Mum!” Her eyes looked like dinner plates.

"By Jingo, Mrs Wheeldon," Ivy said. "You've got a real bad mole problem, haven't you?"

Stupidly, Lou followed their gaze before it dawned on her that the molehills were the heaps of soil she'd emptied earlier.

Next morning, Nicky said, “Mum, you’d better look out on the front lawn.”

Lou opened the front door, and couldn’t believe what she saw.

There must've been at least twenty molehills, ordinary sized ones, on the grass.

"I can hardly believe it. There wasn't any sign of the little gentlemen in black velvet yesterday," Lou said.

"Who are the little gentlemen in black velvet, Mum?" Nicky was puzzled.

"That's what my dad used to call moles. The farmers and workers often wore trousers made out of mole skins. They were like black velvet, and kept the cold out," Lou said.

"Yuk. What a revolting thing to do," said Nicky.

"Times were hard, and moles were plentiful," said Lou.

I'll deal with the breakfast things, then I'll

get out there and clear them up. I'm not sure how we'll stop them, though.

My uncle used to swear by sticking a child's windmill into the molehill. He said the moles didn't like the vibration of the windmill going round, so they'd move on.

I wonder if Strutts have any in their shop, or if I'll have to go into town to buy some."

"Sorry, Mum. I have to go now, or I'll miss the school bus. Good luck with the mole and the molehills." Nicky picked up her lunch and put it in her school bag.

Ivy had saved Nicky a space on the bus.

As Nicky sat down, Ivy began laughing.

"What's the joke?" Nicky asked.

"Is your mum hopping mad this morning?"

asked Ivy.

"She's certainly not pleased. You know we thought those heaps of soil were molehills? Well, this morning, there are loads of real molehills all over the front lawn. Mum's going to try sticking children's windmills into them, so the moles go away."

Ivy laughed even louder.

"C'mon. Spill. What's so funny?" Nicky looked straight at Ivy.

"Last night, I told Mum and Dad about the enormous molehills. Dad said wouldn't it be funny if they encouraged a real mole.

A bit later, Mum said what a joke it would be if we went to yours after dark and put heaps of soil on the front lawn, like molehills.

So we crept around on your lawn, forming piles of soil from the bags we brought from ours.

I hope your mum forgives us when she finds out," Ivy said.

"Oh, you rats," laughed Nicky. "I'd better ring Mum and let her know before she charges off to town, coz I'm sure Strutts won't have any windmills in their shop." Nicky pulled her phone from her pocket.

"Hi, Mum. Yes, it's Nicky. Yes, I'm fine.

Ivy says you might like to just get the soil up with a trowel. She doesn't think they're real molehills." Nicky grinned as she quickly hit the 'call end' button.

Golden Breakfast

"Hola mi amigo!"

"Hey! Gringo! What the fur and feather are you squawking about?"

"It is a beautiful day, eh Apollo? Come, amigo, you and I, we venture forth in search of adventure."

"Well I am not going ANYwhere until I have had breakfast. That is final." Apollo again bent his head to the grass.

"Apollo, you are nothing but a lazy, grey donkey who thinks only of his stomach. I will fetch old Jack to feed you, then we go, eh?"

With a flash of green and red, Gringo was gone.

"That crazy parrot," thought Apollo. *"Every day the same speech about searching for adventure. He knows we are not going on an adventure today or any other day."*

"Señor Jack, Squaawwwkk. Apollo, Él tiene mucha hambre."

"Gringo, you daft parrot, you know I don't understand Spanish, Mexican or whatever you squawk. Squawk in English.

Anyway, I don't have time to talk now, its Apollo's breakfast time."

Throwing open the wooden gate, Jack clanked the metal pail, announcing the arrival of

Apollo's breakfast.

Apollo walked over to the old man, gently nuzzling his arm.

"Hello old fella. I've brought you carrots to clean your teeth." Jack patted Apollo's neck.

Apollo chewed appreciatively.

Suddenly he let out a loud "EEYYORRE", spitting out the carrot.

"What's up old boy? You usually love your carrots."

"Usted me asustó, you scared me! Whatever is the matter with you, idiot donkey?" Gringo settled his ruffled feathers.

"That's no ordinary carrot! It almost broke my teeth!" Apollo pawed at the half eaten carrot on the ground.

As it turned, a glint of gold shone in the sunlight.

Jack bent to pick it up. “Well I never! What have we here? No wonder you made such a fuss old boy. This here carrot has grown itself around a gold sovereign.”

“Today we do not have to search for adventure! Instead it comes to us!” Gringo flew excitedly around the paddock, squawking a mixture of Spanish, Mexican, and English.

Finally, he settled lightly on Apollo’s back.

“Jack, dig deep among the carrots. That is where Señor Paulo he bury the sovereigns.”

“Gringo, you never told me about any sovereigns.”

“When Señor Paulo bring me here on the

ship, he also bring many barrels of brandy.

He sell the brandy for an enormous bag of golden sovereigns.

So big, when he want to bury it in the garden, he have to carry it on the cart!"

Jack picked up a spade and walked purposefully to the vegetable garden.

Apollo eagerly followed, with Gringo sitting on his back, claws entwined in Apollo's thick grey mane.

Jack rubbed his stubbly chin. "Now, let's see if you're telling one of your stories, old bird."

"No, Señor Jack. Gringo tells you truth." Gringo ruffled his feathers.

"Do you remember exactly where Paulo buried those sovereigns, Gringo? It seems logical that they're somewhere around the carrots." Jack looked at the parrot then at the garden.

"Gringo not sure. Such long time ago, but he think you stand almost in right place, Señor Jack."

Soon Jack was digging rhythmically, the spade cutting deep into the soil. He set carrots aside as he dug.

"Dig deep, my friend.

My feathers feel you are in right place." Gringo's head danced from side to side.

"Eeeyorrrre." Apollo dug his hoof into the ground.

"What is it, old boy?"

Jack stopped digging and walked over to Apollo.

He stooped to pick something up, smiling

broadly as he did so.

As Jack dug, more and more gold coins glinted in the sun.

"Well done, boys. We've found Señor Paulo's sovereigns! We'll fetch the cart."

Other books by the same author

For the young and young at heart:

Zondor the Magnificent

The Mystery of the Missing Stick

For adults:

Chilling Armchair Tales

More stories coming soon

Flondellior Publications